Women of the Gospels

A journey in nine stories

Paula Gooder

with illustrations by Ally Barrett

CHURCH HOUSE PUBLISHING

Church House Publishing
Church House
27 Great Smith Street
London SW1P 3AZ

Published 2026 by Church House Publishing

British Library Cataloguing in Publication Data

A catalogue record for this book is available from the British Library

ISBN 978 1 78140 526 0

EU GPSR Authorised Representative
LOGOS EUROPE, 9 rue Nicolas Poussin, 17000, LA ROCHELLE, France. E-mail: Contact@logoseurope.eu

Digital photography by Dan Barrett

Design and typesetting by www.penguinboy.net

Praise for *Women of the Gospels*

'In this beautiful book, Paula Gooder combines biblical scholarship with the tender imagination of the storyteller, giving voice to women at the heart of the gospel story who so often remain unheard. These stories invite us not only to see the world of Jesus afresh, but to discover again a Christ who sees, knows, and restores. This is a book to read prayerfully, and to return to often.'

BISHOP EMMA INESON

'[Paula Gooder's] latest stories, which complete a brilliant devotional trilogy of books, have the beguiling and compelling simplicity that only a real expert can bring. I adore how she does not try to gloss over the pain or messiness many of these women would have faced in their daily lives ... '

RACHEL MANN

Praise for *Women of Holy Week*

'As always, Paula Gooder makes us see the biblical text with fresh eyes and challenges us to see beyond our lazy and stereotyping reading ... beautifully-written and illustrated ... '

JANE WILLIAMS

Praise for *Women of the Nativity*

'Ally Barrett's vivid and compelling paintings combine with Paula's story-telling to bring it all to life. It's not just that we feel as though we were there as we read these stories, but that by the end we know through these stories, that the love of God at the heart of them, is there for us.'

MALCOLM GUITE

Paula Gooder is a writer and lecturer in Biblical Studies. She is the author of many popular books, including *Lydia* (2022) and *Phoebe: A Story* (2018) and one of the editors of the Pilgrim Course. Paula is also Canon Chancellor of St Paul's Cathedral, London.

Ally Barrett has worked in theological education as well as parish ministry and enjoys working at the intersection of creativity, faith, wellbeing and sustainability. She is the author of several books and dozens of hymns. Ally is Associate Vicar at Great St Mary's, Cambridge.

Contents

NOTES AND RESOURCES

Introduction

THIS BOOK, *Women of the Gospels*, is the third and final volume in a short series which includes *Women of Holy Week* (2022) and *Women of the Nativity* (2024). Each volume contains nine short stories, and each story imagines life from the perspective of a particular woman. Although we know very little about the lives and experiences of almost all of the women who appear in the Bible, I have used the knowledge I have from years of study as a New Testament scholar to inform my imaginative tellings of their lives.

In the previous two sets of stories, there was a good mix of women who were named in the accounts, alongside those who appeared but were unnamed – and those whose presence isn't even mentioned but who would have been there nevertheless. Of the women featured in this volume, only one (Martha, with her sister Mary) is named in the Gospels. The rest are identified by their origin (the Samaritan woman, the Syrophoenician woman); their relationship to a man (Jairus' daughter, Simon Peter's wife, who – though not mentioned in the Gospels – had to exist because he had a mother-in-law); what they suffered from (the woman with the haemorrhage and the woman who was bent double); or what people said they had done (the woman caught in adultery).

The one exception is the widow of Nain, whose story reverses the normal trend. Here the son is known only in relation to his mother, the widow, and – although she isn't named – alongside Jesus, she remains the key protagonist of the account.

Since no names are given to these eight women in the Gospels, I have chosen names that were well known and well used in Galilee and Judea in this period. For the Samaritan woman I have used the name given to her in Orthodox Christianity (Photini) and for the Syrophoenician woman the name of a famous Tyrian princess, Elissa (known in Latin texts as Dido), who, according to legend, founded the city of Carthage in North Africa. The only other choice worthy of comment at this point is Tabitha. For Jairus' daughter, as you will see, I allowed myself a flight of fancy and imagined that the girl's name, Tabitha, could be easily mistaken for the Aramaic word for little girl, '*talitha*', which is how Jesus addresses her.

Like the two preceding books, this collection features wonderfully evocative paintings of the individual women by Ally Barrett. For this the final book in this series, Ally and I decided to add an extra story and picture at the end (see page 71). We wanted to imagine a scene in which all these women met at the end of Jesus' life and told their stories to the 'daughters of Jerusalem' to whom Jesus spoke on the way to the cross (Luke 23.27-31).

I would be the first to acknowledge that this is fanciful and unlikely to have happened. It is worth noting, however, that a number of women had travelled to Jerusalem from Galilee and were present at the crucifixion. Although some are named – Mary Magdalene (Matthew 27:56, Mark 15:40, John 19:25), Mary the mother of Jesus (John 19.25), Mary wife of Clopas (John 19.25), Salome (Mark 15.40) and the mother of James and John (Matthew 27.56) – both Matthew and Mark also note that there were other women there, too ('there were many other women who had come up with him to Jerusalem (Mark 15.41); and see also Matthew 27.55). Since the women imagined in this volume and the women mentioned at the crucifixion are unnamed, I see no reason why we shouldn't join them into a single group at such a crucial moment.

At the back of the book, you will find notes for each story. Each section of notes contains one or more Bible passages that can be read alongside the stories, together with some questions to prompt reflection and conversation if you are studying these stories in a group. In addition, for each story, I have provided a few additional notes drawn from scholarship which might make sense of some of the decisions that I have made and which, I hope, will give you some additional background to aid in your own imaginings of the stories.

One of the themes that comes through very powerfully in all of these stories is how isolating illness was for anyone at the time of Jesus. The precarious nature of existence, alongside the purity codes that existed in this period, left people – and especially women – vulnerable and alone when illness struck. Important as healing was in a world before much functional medicine, even more valuable was the restoration to relationship that healing enabled. Jesus gave back to people more than merely their health: healing led to renewed relationships and reintegration into society. Another strand that emerges (particularly from the stories of the Samaritan woman and the woman caught in adultery) is how dependent women were on the judgements that society made about them. As was the case for many centuries even after the time of Jesus, a woman's reputation could be destroyed by a single act of foolishness – sometimes even by a single unfounded story told about her. Similar kinds of judgements continue to be made today, even though our worldview has changed dramatically. For example, commentators still assume that it was the Samaritan woman's fault that she had had five husbands and was not married to the man she then lived with – despite the fact that women could not initiate divorce at the time of Jesus (they could only be divorced if that was initiated by a man). As in the other books in this series, my intention in writing is to bring women's lives out of the shadows. What I see of Jesus' interactions with women in the Gospels reminds me of the story of Hagar in the Old Testament. After she was treated cruelly by Sarah, and ran away into the wilderness, Hagar was met by an angel of the Lord, who told her that she had conceived a child (Genesis 16.7-16). Hagar then named God *'El Roi'* which translates as 'the God of seeing' or 'the God who sees me'. In all the different stories of this book, what comes through is the fact that Jesus saw. He saw women in the lives that they lived. In a world that often overlooked and ignored women, Jesus saw them. In some ways, I would argue that this was even more important than their healing and restoration to society.

The Jesus who saw, still sees today. As you read this book, whatever your background, your experiences, your gender, I pray that you will know yourself to be seen and loved by the Jesus who sees, knows and loves you for exactly who you are.

Paula Gooder
St David's Day, 2026

About the Paintings

Ally Barrett

PROVIDING THE ARTWORK FOR THIS SERIES of books has been a huge and wonderful learning curve. I have learned so much about the art of illustration, about the lives of women in the time of Jesus (often challenging my uncritical assumptions), and most of all about the way that telling and retelling stories – and engaging imaginatively with Scripture (including through art) – can help us grow in faith and deepen our relationship with God in Christ.

The common thread that ties these paintings together is their focus on the relationship between Jesus and those he encounters. As Paula writes in her Introduction, when these women met Jesus, they knew that they had been seen for who they were. In the paintings I tried to show something of this quality of encounter. That's why, when Jesus meets and heals Rebekah, he kneels down so that he can look her in the eye – something she would not have experienced in years.

In these paintings and stories, we see Jesus meeting women where they are, at their point of greatest need, and transforming their lives. So, when we imagine in the Epilogue that the women in the stories meet in Jerusalem to line the way that Jesus would walk, carrying his cross, they are not only sharing their stories with each other and with the 'Daughters of Jerusalem'. They are also telling their stories back to Jesus, reminding him of the resurrections that he has already brought about in them.

At his point of need, they meet him where he is. Photini brings him the water. Mary and Martha show him their relationship restored. Rebekah now stands tall and strong. And Tamar returns his message of *'hesed'* (steadfast love), writing in the dust her message for him on behalf of them all.

For, in this moment, they come together to offer back to Jesus the love that he showed them.

THE STORIES

One

Simon Peter's wife

LEAH'S STORY

My name is Leah. You won't have heard of me. You may never even have thought about me. Though if you think about it now, you do know I existed.

If Peter had a mother-in-law, he must have had a wife. That's me: Peter's mother-in-law's daughter.

You might find it easier to call me Leah.

I married Simon (that was his name when I married him) when I was little more than a girl and he a strapping young man, learning his trade with his brother Andrew.

Simon and Andrew were skilled fisherman, the best in all of Capernaum and Bethsaida. They knew just when to take the boat out, just when to cast the net over the side. There was many a night that they had gone out in the boat, caught a full catch, come back to shore and folded and mended their nets. All while most of the other boats were still out on the lake, the fisherman peering hopefully into the dark waters below.

I'm not saying our life was easy, but it was good enough. Fish prices were high. The Romans couldn't get enough of our sweet, flaky Tilapia, which, when you char it just right over an open fire, melts deliciously on the tongue. Simon even built us our own house in Capernaum, right on the shores of the lake, a few paces away from the synagogue. It was bigger than all our neighbours' houses and comfortably big enough for my mother to join us after my father died.

We did all right. Even in the winter months and we never lacked for something to eat – so long as you didn't mind fish.

But then, one day, it all changed.

WE HEARD OF HIM BEFORE we ever saw him. In a small town like ours, news travels fast. Someone called Jesus just turned up one day and started saying that God's kingdom was near and that we should repent and believe.

He'd come from Nazareth, we heard. My mother and I would joke that he'd bored the few residents of that tiny town witless, so he had to move on and find new people. It used to be funny – until one of those new people was my Simon.

One night Simon went out to fish and the next day he didn't come home from mending his nets, and neither did Andrew.

At first, we feared the worst. It didn't matter how skilful a fisherman you were. If the wind turned and whipped up storm, and you were in the middle of the lake, your boat would be swamped in no time. Our boats were sturdy and broad-bottomed, designed so they wouldn't tip over in a gust of wind. They were also built to hold large shoals of the fish after the catch. But, if the waves grew high and started beating into the boat, there wasn't much you could do, apart from praying that the God who saved Jonah would save you, too. There are far too many Galilean widows in our town whose husbands had got caught in a storm and sank beneath the waves.

So, when he didn't come home, of course, I assumed that the worst had happened. We hurried out, my mother and I, to the shoreline to see if we could find out what had happened. We met Zebedee's wife Hannah who told us everything.

'They've lost all sense,' she said. 'They have gone off after that wandering preacher. You know – that new one from Nazareth.'

Apparently, Jesus had passed by early that morning. Simon and Andrew were coming ashore after a long night's fishing. It had been a hard night and even they had caught nothing. Just at that moment, the sun glinted on a silvery shoal to the right of the boat and they cast their net over the side. As they did so, Jesus called out,

'Here, follow me.'

And they did.

THEY LEFT THEIR NETS right there in the water, hopped over the side of the boat, splashed through the shallows to Jesus and followed him.

'Zebedee saw it all happening,' Hannah told us. 'You know, he moors his boats a little way along from Simon and Andrew.'

I did know. Simon had often complained that Zebedee had stolen the best spot on the lake for mooring boats, the one where the boats were most sheltered from the weather. Simon would often talk about it and how one day he would find a way to get that spot for his and Andrew's boat.

Hannah continued:

'Jesus walked along to where James and John had started mending their nets, and before Zebedee could say a word, Jesus had called to James and John, too. And up they got and went as well. Just like that. No explanation. No apology. They just went.

'What are we going to do, Leah? How are we going to live without them? What will become of us … ?'

On and on Hannah talked, while I stood there on the lake shore trying to make sense of it all.

When Simon eventually deigned to come home, he was different. His eyes shone. He stood taller, looked happier.

But I didn't notice that at the time.

I was too busy shouting.

We took turns my mother and I, but our words glanced off him as though he barely noticed them.

'Call me Peter,' he said. 'The rock – it's my new name'.

I called him other things, and he smiled – smiled, I ask you!

'Jesus said he'd come to set families against each other,'

he told us calmly as he walked out the door.

One day, not long afterwards, my mother came in shiny with sweat from the marketplace.

'You'll never guess what that Jesus has said now,' she said, breathlessly.

I didn't even try.

Apparently, Aaron, our town's scribe, had nobly offered to follow Jesus. Jesus should have been grateful – that priestly family can trace their roots all the way back to the first Aaron – but was he? Of course not.

Aaron's father had just died and all he wanted to do was bury him. Aaron was his only son – there was no one else. It would take him a while to obey all the rituals, but after that he was fully prepared to follow Jesus. What an honour to have someone like Aaron joining his ragbag group.

But Jesus just said, 'Let the dead bury their own dead,' and continued on his way.

When she'd finished telling me this, my mother sank down onto a bench. At first I thought she was overwhelmed by the horror of it all. But it turned out she wasn't.

The sweat on her brows wasn't from the hot summer's day. It was from a fever that quickly took hold. I sat with her day and night, but she got worse and worse. I sat with her day and night, mopping her brow with wet cloths, talking to her of our happiest memories, willing her back to me, but nothing worked.

The house closed in around me, the darkness pressing in on me as I watched her begin to slip away.

I FELT HIS PRESENCE before I saw him.

The darkness shifted behind me as though pressed outwards by a light.

One moment the house was silent, save for my mother's rasping breath, the next it was full. I barely noticed.

A hand reached over my shoulder and touched her hand.

She sat up, just like that.

I turned and there was Jesus, looking at me, his eyes twinkling, and in that moment all my anger and pain melted away. In that moment I understood. Here was light. Here was love and wholeness. Who wouldn't follow when he called?

WE COOKED UP A FEAST that day, my mum and I.

Peter (yes, all right, I started calling him that) and his new friends laughed at us, asking if we were expecting the whole village. To be fair, I did use three measures of flour for the bread. But Jesus didn't laugh. He looked at me – right at me – and signalled that I should sit at his feet with the others like I was actually one of his disciples.

'The kingdom of heaven,' he said, 'is like yeast that a woman took and mixed with three measures of flour until all of it was leavened.'

Then he smiled at me.

Peter looked sheepish. But I sat a little taller in my place.

YOU WON'T HAVE HEARD of me.

After today, chances are you will never think of me again. But that doesn't matter at all.

There is someone who knows me – who really knows me – and that will always be enough.

Two

The Samaritan woman

PHOTINI'S STORY

My name is Photini. I've lived in Sychar for many years now.

My first husband brought me here from Shechem when we got married and here I've been ever since.

I've grown to love this place. When I look north, I can see Mount Ebal's comforting presence, pointing upwards to heaven. If I look south there is Mount Gerizim, the most holy mountain, stretching high above me.

Some days these great mountains feel as though they are my defence against a world that hates me.

I may have grown to love this place, but it hasn't grown to love me.

My heart has been broken five times over here. Not to mention the countless daily slights and wounds.

My first three husbands died of fever. One day they were hale and hearty, the next they were dead.

The people of the village started muttering about me, saying I was cursed. I began to wonder if they were right. Surely no one could be that unlucky that often?

Then it got worse.

My fourth and fifth husbands were brutal and arrogant. They didn't die – though in my darker moments I have to confess I wished they would. I agreed to marry each of them out of desperation. My father was long dead, and no one else cared about me.

But I quickly discovered that there are worse forms of

desperation than being alone.

I was never enough for either of them. I wasn't as beautiful as they thought I should be. The food I cooked was never right. The house was never clean enough.

All day long the criticisms landed, first in my ears and then in my heart.

At least the fourth husband divorced me honestly, he just didn't like the look of me, he said in the written document.

It was the fifth one that really turned the tide against me. He said that I had been unfaithful. When I protested, he said I'd always been a liar.

Of course, the villagers all sided with him. Why wouldn't they? I was an outsider, clearly cursed. Some even 'remembered' seeing me with other men, though when I challenged them their memories became vague.

If I could live on my own I would. But my dowry is long gone, and without a man I have no money, no house and no future.

We agreed, Eleazar and I, that I was clearly not suited to marriage. We weren't even sure if I could marry a sixth time and had no appetite to visit a priest to find out.

He was elderly and tired and needed someone to care for him and his home. He needed looking after more than he cared about the gossip that followed me around like a cloud. I was young but no less tired than him.

It works for us, if not for anyone else, but since they rarely speak to me, that matters little.

I GO TO THE WELL at midday.

It saves the discomfort standing in the full glare of people's displeasure. The heat of the midday sun more than makes up for avoiding the stares and the whispers of a village turned against me.

Sometimes I like to sit there for a while, even in that heat, and imagine Jacob meeting Rachel there. What if one day I could meet someone by the well. Someone who would love me and know me like Jacob knew Rachel?

One day maybe, who knows?

I went to the well yesterday at my usual time.

The sun was beating down relentlessly and I was tired even before I collected the water. I had my head down as I walked and didn't notice the man sitting by the well until the last moment.

I started with surprise. He was sitting in my favourite spot. Was he waiting for me just like I dreamed? I looked again and chuckled at my fanciful foolishness. Look at his clothes, he was clearly Jewish. He wasn't waiting for me at all.

So, what was he doing here? He looked worn out, as though he couldn't have taken another step. Beads of sweat stood out on his head. His lips were cracked. His head hung low. He turned.

'Give me a drink,' he said.

I felt uneasy. Maybe it was a trick. Maybe he'd come

here to kidnap me … or worse. (You heard stories of 'those Jews' and what they liked to do to poor Samaritan women.)

I played for time, my eyes narrowed suspiciously.

'Why would you, a Jew, ask a drink from me, a Samaritan?

His answer had me bemused.

'If you knew God's gift, you'd ask me for living water.'

I said the first thing that came into my head.

'You haven't got a bucket. The well goes down and down. How on earth are you going to get to the water?'

He started talking about how people who drank of this water would never be thirsty again.

That sounded nice. Imagine never having to come out here at midday ever again? I had a sneaking feeling, though, that I was missing something, but I couldn't work out what it was.

'Give me this water,' I said, 'then I won't have to come here anymore.'

'Why don't you call your husband,' he said, 'and come back?'

He was looking at me, then, like he could see right into my heart. I flushed deep red but there was no point trying to hide it.

'I haven't got a husband.'

What he said next made me sink to the ground right next to him.

'No, the man you have now isn't your husband, is he? And you had five before that.'

I lowered my head, ready for the onslaught. He must

have met someone on the way, who'd told him everything and he'd waited here specially to humiliate me.

I took a deep breath and waited.

BUT THE ONSLAUGHT never came.

Instead, there was a deep, comforting silence that somehow wrapped itself around me. I lifted my head hesitantly and on his face was not condemnation, or judgement.

He wasn't despising me. He wasn't even angry. He was looking at me as if … as if he understood everything and loved me, nevertheless.

'Are you a prophet?' I stammered.

And then – as though the floodgates had opened – we talked about everything. The heartbreak and the humiliation. The loneliness and the shame. The hopelessness and fear of what had happened. I'm pleased to say that I gave him a good run for his money. I wasn't going to let this Jew despise my beloved, holy mountain. But he didn't seem to worry much about that, he started talking about worship and how it wouldn't matter where we did it so long as we did it from the heart.

As he spoke, my shrivelled, aching heart blossomed as though he was watering it with the living water he had mentioned. Suddenly I thought I knew who he was. He knew so much about me, about the world, about everything. 'I know the Messiah is coming, he will tell us everything we need to know.'

'I am he,' he said simply.

At that moment, some other Jews arrived bringing bread from the village.

They looked surprised to see us sitting there chatting, but they didn't say anything. Suddenly I knew I had to tell everyone in the village. I ran all the way back, forgetting all about my tiredness. At first, they pulled away, like they always did when I approached. But my heart was too full of excitement to pay much attention.

'You've got to come,' I said, 'I've just met a man who told me everything I've ever done.'

'That's quite a lot,' quipped one of the men.

They all laughed. Usually, I would have withdrawn in shame at that, but my news was too important.

'I think he might be the Messiah,' I said. 'You don't think he could be, do you?'

I had them at that, and they all trailed back after me to the well, even in the midday sun.

THEY INVITED HIM BACK TO THE VILLAGE and he stayed a few days.

Overnight, everyone forgot that they didn't speak to me. And they hung on the man's every word.

Our whole village blossomed, like my heart had done. It was as though he watered us all with that living water he talked about. I would say he did it with his words, but I can't say we understood them all. I think he really watered us all with who he was.

That spring he talked about was inside him and flowed from him to each one of us, coaxing us back to life. People would stop me in the street to tell me that they knew he was the Saviour of the world.

It was a few days after he left that I suddenly remembered: I never had given him that drink.

Three

The woman who bled for twelve years

DINAH'S STORY

My name is Dinah. I grew up in Bethsaida, a few miles away from Capernaum, but moved to Capernaum when I married my husband, Jonathan, which feels like a lifetime ago.

He was a fisherman, like so many others in Capernaum. Not as successful as some – but we did all right. We weren't rich, but we weren't poor either and he taught me how to save the few coins we had left over at the end of a week.

'You never know what might happen,' he would say. 'You never know when we might need a little extra.'

Each week I would smile at him, as I imagined a growing family playing around us, boisterous with their demands and what little extra that might bring.

At first, life was good. We were young. We were healthy. We were happy. Just one thing blotted our lives.

We waited and waited for that family I imagined – but none came.

All around me, the friends I'd grown up with had one baby, then another, then even more. But while their bellies grew round, mine stayed flat. I dreaded my monthly bleeding. Each month, it came without fail. And when it came, it came with such pain that I could barely speak or walk. My kind husband would look at me sadly as I lay on our bed, whimpering with the agony of it.

'Do you think,' he'd whisper (as though he couldn't bear to utter the words), 'do you think you're quite normal? I asked the other husbands, and their wives don't behave like this.'

But the pain was too great, and I was too heartsore to answer him. So, instead I'd turn my face to the wall of our small house until he went away.

AFTER A WHILE I COULDN'T CALL IT my monthly bleeding anymore. It went on longer and started earlier, until there was barely a break before it all started again.

My husband took a pallet and started sleeping near the door, so that he could come in and go out without touching me, without risking becoming unclean. A blanket of silence fell over us. He was at a loss for words, and I was too exhausted to speak.

I couldn't really go out anymore. On the rare occasion I did go out, the blood would flow constantly, leaving little trails of shame behind me on the road. People would step over it with exaggerated strides so that everyone around them would know they had missed it.

And me? Of course, they avoided me, too. They would stop and wait for me to pass, or swerve exaggeratedly, hiding their eyes as though the very sight of me would make them unclean.

It seemed as though someone had drawn an invisible ring around me that no one could cross. I felt as alone as the prophets who wandered by themselves in the desert – only I lived in a village, surrounded by people.

One day, my husband came home with hope in his eyes. 'There's a doctor,' he said, 'in Antioch. He heals women of …'

He waved his hand up and down in my direction. We both knew why. You couldn't call something 'monthly bleeding' if it never stopped.

'We'll go and see him, and he will heal you.'

And so we went, clutching our savings along with our fragile hope.

The doctor made me poultices out of foul-smelling herbs and took our money, but still the blood came.

Next, we went to Jericho. The doctor there gave me bitter herbs to drink. He, too, took our money, but still the blood came.

Then we went Sidon, then to Tiberias, then Hebron. Then I lost track of the places we went to. Each time we went clutching a little less money and lot less hope.

Still the blood came.

In the end, my husband said to me gently, from his pallet by the door, 'I think we've seen all the doctors. There's no one left.'

'No money either,' I agreed with him wearily.

And we turned our backs on hope and went back to our silent, separate lives.

IT WAS JONATHAN'S idea.

He came in from the lake one day much, much later than usual. He'd been listening to a teacher who'd been preaching from a boat on the lake. Apparently, he was a healer, too. When he'd stepped back on shore, there had been a crowd of people pressing around him, clamouring to be healed.

'Why don't we give it one last try?' Jonathan suggested.

I sighed.

'We have no more money.' Though, if I was honest, the real answer was that I had no more hope.

'He doesn't charge,' he responded. 'He's not that kind of healer. If you saw him, you'd see that.'

My reply came out sharper than I'd intended.

'What kind of healer doesn't charge? That shows he's no good.'

'Just go and look at him at least.'

So I did.

I crept out of the house, my cloak held tightly around me, in the hope that no one would know who I was. And I watched him.

I kept my distance, of course, but everyone was so focused on getting close to him that no one noticed a solitary figure, looking on in the distance.

Jonathan was right. This Jesus was different. He was

different from anyone I had ever met – let alone those doctors who had (without exception) looked down on me with contempt as though my bleeding was, somehow, my fault. Despite the crowds pressing around him, Jesus looked at each person he healed as though they were the only person in existence.

I turned to make my way home, thinking hard. The more I thought, the more convinced I became that Jonathan was right. Maybe Jesus was the one who could help.

Over the next few days, I did everything I could to get close to him. But the crowds were too big, and I didn't dare risk touching anyone.

I took to sitting by the lake, watching, hoping that I might find a way to meet him.

Then one day, I was sitting there all alone. And I saw a boat on the horizon. As the boat drew closer, I got to my feet. There was Jesus in the stern, his disciples gathered around him. It looked as though he was telling them something and they were straining to understand. The next moment, he was striding through the shallows onto the beach right next to me, and I opened my mouth to speak.

This was my moment. This was the time I could tell him everything and he would hear, understand and heal me.

But then it all went wrong.

Jairus, the leader of the synagogue, came running down

the beach, a large crowd behind him. He threw himself at Jesus' feet.

'My little daughter is dying! Please come, lay your hands on her so she can live.'

My hopes crumbled before my eyes.

Of course, Jesus went with him. Why wouldn't he? Jairus was wealthy. He was important. And his little daughter was so ill.

I slumped down where I was, feeling utterly defeated.

BUT THEN SOMETHING CHANGED in me – something I hadn't felt in a very long time.

It was a flicker of hope. The merest hint of it, but still it was there.

Why shouldn't I follow him? If he wasn't going to touch me, why shouldn't I touch him?

The crowd were so intent on Jesus' short journey to Jairus' house that no one paid attention to me, wrapped so carefully in my cloak as a I edged closer and closer to him. I dare not think how many people I made unclean in my desperation, but by then I had one thing in mind.

I must touch his cloak. That was all it needed.

The first time I missed. I stretched as far as I could but brushed the air around him but not his actual cloak. So, I stretched again.

This time I touched it with the very tip of just one of

my fingers. As I did, I felt a tingle travel up my arm, and down into my body. And just like that, the searing cramps stopped.

I had just had time to notice this when Jesus turned and asked who'd touched him.

The disciples tried to tell him that it was everyone and no one in the crowd, but he knew -and I knew – that they were wrong.

I stumbled towards him and fell at his feet, shaking all over.

My cloak fell back, revealing my face and the crowd drew back in horror. I barely noticed. Right there on the ground in front of everyone I told him everything – the bleeding and the pain, the loneliness and the fear, the doctors and the money. It all came tumbling out of me.

He reached down and held my hand and drew me to my feet. I could feel his skin on mine. It was the first time I had felt human touch in twelve long years.

'Daughter,' he said, breaking into my incoherent ramblings, 'daughter, your faith has saved you. Go – live in peace and be whole'.

As he did so, he glanced up and over my shoulder. There was Jonathan standing behind me, beaming his joy.

AND SO, WE ARE TRYING, Jonathan and I, to *be* whole.

Some days are better than others. Twelve years of silence

and separation take their toll.

But every day we give thanks for Jesus of Nazareth. Every day we resolve to do as he commanded: to live in peace and be whole.

Four

Jairus' daughter

TABITHA'S STORY

My name is Tabitha. Capernaum is my home. I know every last inch of the village.

I know the beaches where the water laps the shore, accompanying the shouts of the fishermen as they come back home with their catch.

I know the two roads in and out of the village and the traders who travel them, their packs bulging with exotic goods to be taken to places I couldn't even dream of.

I know the olive groves and vineyards stretching up the hillside away from the lake, where labourers work hard in the sun day in and day out.

I know everyone in the village, too. I know who to speak to and who to stay away from. I stay away from the Romans – everyone knows that – and also those tax-collectors who sit in their booths and make the traders curse with their exorbitant demands.

I stay away from the sinners, too, like my Abba says I should.

'What did they do,' I would ask my Abba, 'to make them sinners?'

He would shake his head disapprovingly.

'That's not for you to know,' he would say, and I learned not to add 'But why?' because he would grow stern and distant, and I didn't like it when he was stern and distant. Instead, I asked it on the inside. One day I'll find the answer to my question.

I also stay away from the woman Dinah.

'She's unclean,' my father once told me. 'She bleeds.'

'Did she cut herself?' I'd asked.

But he'd grown stern and distant again, and I learned that this was another question to ask on the inside.

My Abba is a very important man. He runs the synagogue.

I tell my friends he is the most important man in the whole of Capernaum. When he hears me, he smiles, and I can tell he is pleased. But then he reminds me that he runs the synagogue with two others. He's only one of the leaders of the synagogue, he says.

I shrug and take no notice. To me he is – and always will be – the most important man in the whole of Capernaum.

Some days, he lets me go with him to the synagogue. I smooth the curtain in front of the Torah. I sweep the floors to keep them clean. I make myself as helpful as possible.

On very special days, Abba teaches me to find the place in the Torah for the reading. I'm a fast learner and I'm learning to see the shapes of the letters. I can nearly read all the words without help.

I tell Abba that one day I'd like to be the person who reads in the assembly, and he looks at me with love, strokes my cheek and tells me that can't be. This makes me indignant. I can read better than all the boys my age. He agrees but says again that it just can't be.

The other day I was tracing the letters with my finger and saying the words out loud as I did - it was my favourite story of Miriam and baby Moses in the bulrushes – when Abba's brow creased.

'You haven't started bleeding, have you?'

I looked down at my knee. I had tripped when I was playing games yesterday. A scab was forming right there on the top of my knee.

'My knee's all right, look!' I showed him.

He looked relieved and gave a little laugh.

'That's all right then. You're still my little daughter.'

I was confused. It felt as though he was asking me something else. But I didn't know what it was, and he looked stern and distant again. So, I said nothing.

Why would it matter so much if my knee was bleeding? I resolved to ask Imma when I got home.

I NEVER DID ASK HER because when I got home, I felt suddenly hot and tired.

Imma took one look at me and sent me to bed.

That night I felt feverish. My dreams were full of words floating around and changing shape before I had time to read them.

Whenever I opened my eyes, Imma's face floated above me, anxiety written all over her face.

'Sleep, dear one,' she said. 'In the morning you will feel better.'

But in the morning I was not better.

I was hot and miserable, and it felt as though someone or something was sitting on my chest so that I could barely breathe.

Day and night blended into one and I drifted in and out of terrifying dreams.

The house was quiet all around me and all I saw were the fearful faces of Imma and Abba looking down at me. They felt very far away, and I felt myself drifting into a deep sleep.

At some point I became aware – to my surprise – that at last my chest had stopped hurting. There was also a strange rattling noise that came whenever I breathed.

Just before I was sucked into sleep, I heard Abba saying that he was going to get Jesus, the teacher from Nazareth.

I also heard Imma replying that she thought he was too late. She'd sent for the mourners already.

And then all was black, quiet and peaceful.

THE NEXT THING THAT I KNEW, a voice I didn't know was calling to me.

It was a beautiful voice – gentle and full of love.

'*Tabitha, cum*,' he said.

It was what Imma said to me every morning as I woke from sleep: 'Tabitha, get up.'

So, I did.

I sprang out of bed and ran to my Imma, as I did every morning.

Imma gave a cry of delight. She wrapped her arms around me as though she would never let me go and sobbed as though her heart would break.

'What is it, Imma?' I asked, worried.

I didn't like it when Imma cried. It felt as though my sunny, steady world became wobbly and unstable.

'I thought you were dead,' she sobbed, 'but then the teacher saved you.'

I turned and there was a man I'd seen down by the shore with crowds all around him and three of the fishermen. I used to watch them as they counted their catch and mended their nets.

The teacher spoke then. He said something about not telling anyone about what had happened. But I recognised his voice. It was the voice that had told me to get up.

I took a step forward.

'How did you know my name?' I asked.

'He didn't,' Imma explained hurriedly, in her way that told me I wasn't to ask anything else. 'He said the word talitha – little girl. He didn't say your name.'

I looked at him uncertainly and he winked. His face as full of love as his voice had been.

All at once, I knew that he knew more about me than just my name. He knew everything about me. He was someone who would never make me ask questions on the inside.

'I think Tabitha is hungry,' he said to Imma.

And suddenly I realised I was. I have never been so hungry as I was then. Imma bustled away to prepare a feast such as I had never had before or since.

Jesus reclined on one of the couches by the table and gestured that I should recline right next to him, like a grown up.

'Now,' he said, 'you look like you might be someone who has a lot of questions.'

And we sat next to each other, the teacher and I, and we asked each other questions until the evening came.

As he left that evening, he bent down and whispered in my ear: 'Blessed are those who hunger and thirst for righteous, for they will be filled.

'Never stop asking questions, little one.'

And so I never have.

Every time my Imma and Abba told the story after that – and they told it a lot – they'd say that the teacher had said '*talitha, cum.*'

But I know, whatever they think, that he called me by my name.

After all, he knew everything about me … and every last question I asked on the inside.

Five

The Syrophoenician woman

ELISSA'S STORY

My name is Elissa. I live in Tyre, the most beautiful city in the world.

I haven't travelled anywhere else, but the merchants who pass by on the great trading road assure me that it is.

They come with their tales of Egypt and Judea, Galilee and Syria, and I listen as they paint pictures in my mind of lands far away.

As they speak, I imagine the grand pyramids of Egypt, the glorious Temple in Jerusalem, the hustle and bustle of Damascus. I see all these places in my mind's eye and then I can't help agreeing that Tyre really is the most beautiful city in the world.

When their tales are finished, they bring out spices and incense, tapestries and carpets, glassware and pots. Sometimes I reward them for their tales with a purchase before I call my husband.

That's the real reason that they come.

We, like our neighbours, make the finest purple dyes. The traders will take them to the great courts in Damascus and Egypt and Jerusalem and sell them for four or five times what we charge. One trader has contacts in the court of Herod Antipas; another sells to the Roman Pontius in Jerusalem.

They are always eager to buy, though they try to hide this beneath their polished tales and elaborate gestures. The more desperate my husband knows them to be, the higher the price goes.

One day, my daughter came out as one of the traders was spreading out his wares.

She doesn't leave the house much anymore.

When she was a small child, I left a pot of water uncovered one evening. I didn't notice until I saw her standing on tiptoes trailing her fingers in its coolness and then licking them one by one. I called out in horror, terrified that a water demon might be hiding on the water's surface. At first, all was well. I watched her like a hawk for signs of blindness or convulsions or madness, but she was her usual happy self, playing on the sea shore where we collected the murex snails, making mounds out of shells and chattering cheerfully to herself.

It was only about six months later that I began to see the change in her.

To begin with, she would suddenly fall silent, her eyes flickering unseeingly for a few moments before she began her play again. But the demon that had lain quietly in her at the start began to strengthen its grip.

Soon she would fall to the ground, clutching her head, her limbs jerking uncontrollably or she would sit in the shadows of our house, barely speaking at all with her lips making the shapes of words that never emerged.

She barely slept and would wander for miles along the sea front alone – save for the demon within.

Little by little we were losing her to the demon and

there was nothing we could do about it.

THE TRADER HAD LOOKED at her slack face – her lips mouthing words no one but the demon could hear – and he turned to me, a sympathetic look on his face.

'Has a demon got her?'

I nodded, not trusting myself to speak, and bent over his wares so that he wouldn't see the tears that had sprung into my eyes. Still, one large single tear fell onto the glass he was showing me and slid its sorrowful way down to its base.

'You should take her to the healer from Galilee,' he said. 'He arrived in the city in the group I was travelling with from Capernaum.'

He started telling me about this Jesus from Nazareth and how he healed the sick and made bread enough for thousands. How he was annoying the religious leaders with his teaching, and how the crowds that followed him hung on his every word.

I shook my head.

'The demon is too strong. It would be no use.'

Then he told me of a man from the Decapolis, the cities on the other side of Galilee.

'He had more demons than anyone I've ever heard of,' the merchant said. 'He had so many demons they called themselves Legion. But they were no match for this Jesus: he dispatched them into a herd of pigs!'

'Do you think I could?' I asked the trader.

'What have you got to lose?'

At that point my husband emerged from the workshop, reeking of the smells of dye-making, so I was glad to turn away and go in search of my daughter.

With every step that I took, my determination grew stronger.

I would take her. Jesus would heal her. All would be well.

BUT SHE WOULDN'T come. Every time I took her hand, she pulled away, silently shaking her head. I could see the demons forming her lips into the word 'no' over and over again.

So, I left her, huddled in the kitchen and stumbled towards the marketplace, numb with grief. There is nothing so crushing as having a glimmer of hope snatched from your hands before it has even had time to catch alight.

I saw him at the end of the street, going into the house belonging to a Jew who lived there, a crowd of Galileans around him. I don't know how I knew it was him. It might have been the rough-looking Galileans (they stick out like a sore thumb in these more cultured parts) – but I don't think it was.

As soon as I saw him, I knew deep within me that it was him and that I had to make him help me.

Looking back on it now, I can't believe what came over me.

I pushed my way into the house just as he'd settled down on a couch by the table with a long weary sigh.

I fell on my knees before Jesus, my hands clutched to my chest and poured out my story, begging him to help me.

'But where is your daughter?' asked one of the Galileans that had arrived with him. 'Didn't you want to bring her?'

'She wouldn't come,' I replied, and hung my head in hopelessness.

I was wrung out and stayed there on my knees before Jesus, waiting to hear what he would say.

'Let the children be fed first,' he said. 'It is not fair to take the children's food and throw it to the dogs.'

Everyone in the house gasped. I winced.

We know they think we are dogs, but it's not every day you hear it said out loud – and to your face. I sagged. I had screwed up every last bit of nerve I had in me to come here, and wasn't quite sure what to do now.

At that moment, I saw a movement out of the corner of my eye. It was one of those ever-present scrawny scavenger dogs that must have crept in with the crowd, working its way backwards and forwards under the table, licking up every crumb it could find.

My courage returned. I lifted my head defiantly.

'Lord,' I said, 'even the dogs under the table eat the children's crumbs.'

I nodded my head in the dog's direction.

He turned and looked. His eyes twinkled as he looked back at me. He nodded as though he understood me.

'You spoke well,' he said. 'The demon has left your daughter.'

And that was it.

Only a few sentences passed between us – between me and this man who changed my life for ever – but with them passed a deep current of understanding.

I saw him in all his weariness and exhaustion. He saw me in my terror and desperation. He nodded at me and I at him, and then I left.

WHEN I GOT HOME, I found my daughter in bed fast asleep. She stirred as I entered.

'Imma!' she cried, and flew to my arms in a way she had not done for years.

When I told my husband about it all later, he asked:

'Weren't you shocked by his rudeness?'

'I don't know,' I said. 'I can't work out if it was what he really thought or if he was tired and in a bad mood. He might, even, have been wanting me to say something back to him, which I did. It didn't seem important at the time, and now … '

I turned to look at our daughter, who was piling up sea

shells on the shore and pealing with laughter every time they toppled over.

'Now it doesn't matter at all.'

Six

The widow of Nain

JUDITH'S STORY

My name is Judith. I live in Nain. It is a village that lives up to its name: 'lovely'.

There is no other word for it. It is lovely. Its fields are green, its soil rich.

The olives and vines we grow on the slopes of Mount Moreh are better than anyone's for miles around. Sometimes I pause from my work tending the vines or picking the olives and look out over the valley of Jezreel. It stretches out from our village all the way to Mount Carmel in the distance. Field upon field of rich fertile land.

Surely there could be no place more beautiful than Nain?

A little north of us is another small village, called Nazareth. We get lots of news from there.

A year or so ago, I heard rumours that one of their sons had gone quite mad. He had left home and started teaching. Apparently, he spoke as though he thought he had authority – or so they say – but he was only Joseph and Mary's son.

He'd never trained with anyone as far as I know. Jesus, his name was.

Mary had even gone once to try and bring him home, to stop him bringing so much shame on their family. He'd refused, looked around at the crowd he was talking to, and called them his mother and brothers and sisters instead.

The horror of it! It must have broken his poor mother's heart.

WHEN I HEARD the terrible tale, I looked over at my own son, Nathan.

He was my gift from God. He lit up my life with joy. He would never treat me like that. My Nathan was everything to me.

A few years ago, my beloved husband died. He had been in the vineyard, pruning the vines, like his father had taught him (and his father before that). The day labourer who came running to break the news told me that one moment he had been talking to the vines, telling them where he was going to cut (he said it made them grow better) – the next moment, he had given an odd grunt and fallen to the ground. He never woke again.

It was a few years ago now, but by then Nathan was a man. He took over running the olive grove and vineyard that had been in my husband's family for generations.

Together we tended the trees and the vines. When the olives had been pressed and the wine matured, he would take our produce off to market far north in Sepphoris, ensuring we got the best prices for everything he sold.

We were a team, Nathan and I. No, he would never have treated me, like poor Mary's son had treated her.

He was the sweetest, kindest, most hard-working son a

mother could ask for. I gave thanks every morning for my life with my boy. There was nothing more I could wish for in all the world.

THE DISASTER, WHEN IT CAME, was as sudden as it was devastating.

Nathan had gone into the watchtower in our vineyard. It was used day and night, as one of us would sit there watching diligently to make sure our precious crops were safe from harm. One of the day labourers had come earlier that day to say that they thought one of the boards was rotten. Nathan had gone to look at it. The labourer was right. The rotten board gave way beneath Nathan's weight. He plunged to his death below – and with him fell my whole life.

In a single moment, I went from having everything I could wish for in the world to having nothing. Nothing at all.

My husband was dead. My beloved son was gone. The olive grove and vineyard would go to my husband's brother. I would most likely be turned out onto the streets. My husband's brother and his wife had never liked me. Even in the few hours between Nathan's death and his burial, they'd already started dropping dark hints about the future.

I barely listened. What did I care?

My life had ended when that floorboard cracked. I had nothing left.

THE VILLAGE CAME TOGETHER to arrange Nathan's funeral. They needed to. I could neither speak nor think.

I followed his body as they carried him out of the village to the burial grounds beyond. To the tomb where my husband was buried with his father and his father's father and his father's father's father. My son's bones would rest alongside those of his ancestors.

We had just reached the gates of the village, when we met a man with a large crowd of people behind him. He looked vaguely familiar but, in my grief, I couldn't begin to work out who he was.

'Don't weep,' he said.

I lifted my head to give him a piece of my mind. How dare this stranger tell me not to weep when my life had collapsed around me and I had lost my only, beloved son?

The words never formed in my mouth because, as I lifted my head, I looked into his face. He was looking at me with such compassion that my broken heart fluttered in my chest. It felt as though this person whom I couldn't place saw my torment and anguish ... and not only saw it but felt it himself.

He moved forward and touched the board on which they were carrying my son's broken body and said:

'Young man, I say to you, get up.'

I was about to explain to him what had happened.

Perhaps he didn't understand? Perhaps he hadn't noticed that we were on our way to bury him?

But just then my son sat up and started talking. He asked where we were going and where this crowd had come from. The man signalled to those carrying him that they should lay the board down. And then he brought him to me.

'Woman,' he said, 'here is your son.' The compassion on his face was replaced by pure joy.

I took my son in my arms and wept as though my heart would break. Only this time it wouldn't: my son had been dead and now lived. In a single moment I went from having nothing in the world, to everything I could wish for.

I TURNED BACK TO LOOK at the man – and suddenly recognition dawned.

'Jesus?' I said. 'Little Jesus?'

The memories of him as a child came back to me.

Long before Nathan was born, Joseph – Mary's husband – would come to Nain sometimes to do odd jobs around the village. There was no one to rival his skill in woodwork and building in all the area. Some of the things that Joseph had built were as solid today as the day he finished them.

Sometimes, when he came, he brought Jesus with him. I had forgotten all about it until just now.

Jesus was an odd, serious little child. He would sit watching his father at work, or looking up at the sky or over the valley as if in deep thought. He always looked as though he was thinking about something.

I would ask him sometimes what he was thinking about and he would reply enigmatically, 'My father's business.'

And now here he was standing before me, a grown man. A grown man who had just brought my son back to life.

Jesus shrugged and smiled.

'Not so little now.'

I realised then that those tales I'd heard – the ones that had caused such outrage in me – had missed out something essential. They had overlooked who he was. He did have authority – an authority that was entirely his own. I knew in that moment that I would have followed him anywhere.

He touched my arm.

'Go, live to the full, and be whole.'

I turned – my heart full – and made my way home, Nathan beside me. Thanks to Jesus of Nazareth, we had the whole of our lives before us.

Seven

The woman caught in adultery

TAMAR'S STORY

My name is Tamar. I live in Jerusalem. I haven't always lived here. I grew up in Jericho, among palm trees and desert sands, and moved here when I married my husband a few years ago.

It was a good marriage, my parents told me. They had saved since my birth to provide a dowry that would attract a man like Menahem. He was wealthy, he was influential

'He was *old*,' I thought to myself when I met him, just before our wedding.

When I said so to my father, he threw his head back and laughed.

'He's only thirty-five! Not old at all!'

But, to my fourteen-year-old self, he was as old as the hills.

I also discovered (after the elaborate and lavish wedding) that he was set in his ways.

His previous wife Naomi had died, and he was looking for someone to replace her: to be exactly as she was (only a bit better).

He had a long list of qualities I needed to adopt to achieve this state. I tried hard to live up to the person he wanted me to be, but time and time again I failed. I wasn't graceful enough. I didn't run the household as he wanted. I didn't greet his important guests in quite the right way.

Almost every day I heard the phrase, 'What Naomi used to do was ...'

I hated her so much. Even her name meant 'delightful'. She was perfect in every way … and I? I just wasn't enough.

So, I'm not asking you to understand. I know what I did

was wrong. I'm just explaining why it happened.

I WAS MISERABLE and life seemed hopeless.

Then suddenly … there he was.

Baruch was my husband's secretary. He wrote letters for Menahem, drew up contracts for his business and kept tallies of everything we spent.

I would see him going through the house, making lists. Every day I would meet him somewhere around the house, and every day he would smile at me as though the very sight of me made his day better.

At first, we talked about jars of spice and cups for guests, but soon we fell to talking about ourselves. We shared stories of our lives before we came here. He was the same age as me and we compared our childhoods – mine in Jericho and his in Alexandria. He was lonely. He missed his family and his home.

Soon I began to look for him and would find myself loitering in the parts of the house where I knew he would be. When he saw me, his face lifted and, then, so would my heart.

As I tell you about it all now, you must see how it was going to end. But I was young and innocent and didn't think about what might happen next. Before long I was in love. It wasn't that I didn't know it was wrong. Whenever I thought about it, I would feel flickers of shame. So, I would stop thinking about it and bask instead in the heat of our love.

It was a love that burned as fierce as the midday sun and filled every part of me both day and night. It consumed me so entirely that I forgot to be careful.

Looking back on it now, I wonder whether I wanted to be found out. Wanted or not, Menahem burst in one night when Baruch and I were in bed together. Our secret was out.

I expected Menahem to be furious, but it was worse than that.

He was cool, calm, calculated.

THE NEXT MORNING Baruch had disappeared and was never heard of again. I can only hope that he had been sent back home. I dare not imagine what else might have happened to him.

Late in the morning, I was summoned to the grand entrance hall, where Menahem liked to meet his influential guests. Gathered there was a group of scribes and Pharisees in deep conversation.

As I entered, a hush fell on the room as the whole group turned to look at me. Their faces were full of contempt, as though the stench of rotten flesh had wafted into the room along with me.

'This is her?'

They addressed their question to Menahem. He nodded his agreement.

The shame – which had flickered deep within since

the first moment I had realised that what I was doing was wrong – raged through my body, turning my neck and face crimson.

No one noticed. They weren't looking at me.

'She'll do. Come.'

They turned to me, surrounding me as a group, so that I had no choice but go with them. They took very great care to avoid touching me.

Out of the corner of my eye, I saw Menahem join the back of the group. Clearly, he wanted to watch whatever was going to unfold.

I soon realised that they weren't that interested in me and my shameful secret. They had something else in mind. I was useful to them in a battle I knew nothing about.

As they walked, they discussed what they thought he would do. They seemed to think they were going to trap someone with something and were going to use me to do it.

WE WALKED THROUGH THE STREETS at a fast pace.

After a few minutes, I realised we were going to the Temple. We entered through the Huldah gates into the dimly lit tunnels, before emerging into the full sunlight of the court of the Gentiles.

They searched through the porticos that lined the edges of the Temple until they saw him. At first, I couldn't see him myself. I was still boxed in between them all. But then the group fanned out.

There before me was a man, who from his dress seemed to be from Galilee. From behind me, one of the Pharisees was explaining that I had been caught in an act of adultery and they wondered what he thought should happen to me.

Should I be stoned maybe, like Moses commanded?

I looked round in alarm. We'd all heard the stories of how they used to stone women caught in adultery, but they never actually did it. Did they?

Behind me, the voices of the scribes and Pharisees rose, citing cases, asking questions. I could feel their venom eating into my spine. They talked over one another, creating a wall of noise so loud that I couldn't hear what any one of them said.

In front of me, the man sat on the ground calmy. He let them talk. Peace radiated from him, their fury gliding over him like oil over water.

While their tirade thundered around us, this man leaned forward and wrote something in the sand. The others were too far away to see what it said, but I, from my vantage point, saw the word perfectly. Baruch had taught me to trace out some letters and to learn some verses of the Scriptures by heart. So, I knew immediately that this word was '*hesed*' – steadfast love.

As he finished the final letter, he looked at me right in the eye – the first time anyone had done so all day. In his eyes I saw compassion and understanding, but also a steeliness that I knew meant he expected me to do better, be better.

I held onto my dress, closing it at the neck. In my hurry

to get dressed this morning, I had thrown on the nearest dress to hand. I felt dishevelled and unkempt. I was already ashamed enough without my dress making it worse.

He stood up and said to them:

'Anyone who is without sin, you can cast the first stone.'

Then he sat down again and wrote another word. I knew that one, too: *'emet'* – truth.

I tensed and closed my eyes. I couldn't believe it. He had looked as though he had understood, but now he said they could stone me.

I stood there, my eyes squeezed shut, waiting for the first stone to strike.

BUT NOTHING CAME. I heard a slight rustle but nothing else.

Then I heard his voice again.

'Where are they? Has no one passed a death sentence on you?'

I looked around. All I could see were the backs of the scribes and Pharisees as they scurried away. The back nearest to me was Menahem, who had clearly left last.

'No, sir,' I said, trembling now.

'Then I don't judge you either,' he said. 'Go, and don't sin again.'

And I won't.

I don't know what the future will hold for me now.

I don't know if Menahem will let me back in the house or not. I don't even know if I want him to.

But as I face whatever lies ahead for me, I will carry with me those two words *'hesed'* and *'emet'* – steadfast love and truth – and the memory of his peacefulness.

Eight

The woman who was bent double

REBEKAH'S STORY

My name is Rebekah. I've lived all my life in the small town of Gamla, high up in the mountains overlooking Lake Galilee. And if you stand in just the right spot and crane your neck in just the right way, you can see the lake twinkling in the far distance.

I had always loved that lake, though I'd never been to it.

Father would travel there often, taking our rich, deep-green olive oil to market and returning with fish and tales of life on a lake I could only dream of. Tales of gruff fishermen, their skin weathered by sun and wind; of traders bringing their wares from Egypt to Syria and back again; of tax-collectors insisting on payment even from the most reluctant of traders, and of bandits doing their best to drive those hated Romans from our land.

I spent my childhood looking out to the lake and imagining that one day I would go and see it for myself. Then, I would stand up as tall as I could, imagining myself to be a lofty tree reaching to the heavens, so that I could see as much of the lake as possible, glinting in the sunlight far beneath me.

Until *that* day, it was eighteen years since I had last seen it.

Until *that* day, all I had left were fragments of memories of what I once took for granted. I used to dream of visiting the lake, of dipping my feet in its cool water and sitting on the shore listening as it lapped against the stones.

But then – all at once – I was forced to give up hope even of glimpsing it from the corner of my eye.

Even as a child my back would hurt sometimes. My mother would say that I had strained it with all that stretching upwards to look out over Galilee. I would smile and stretch up a little taller, just to show her that I could.

The pains came in earnest in the year before I was due to marry, and little by little I began to bend like a tree in the wind, only – unlike the trees once the wind had dropped – I never stretched back up again.

Each year I bent a little more. Each year the pain grew worse, until, one day, all I could see was the ground and nothing more.

Gone were the hours of looking out to my beloved Galilee. Gone were the days of scampering up the mountain with the shepherd boys. Gone were the visits to our family olive grove to see how our ancient trees were doing.

All I could do was shuffle from place to place, tracking my progress along the streets I knew so well by the stones and holes in the road.

I thought I had lost everything I loved. No husband would take me on. I lived at home with my parents, my life as stiff and painful as my bent back.

The highlight of my week was to accompany my mother to the women's section of the synagogue and listen to the stories of God's people of old: Abraham and Sarah, Jacob, Rachel and Leah and, of course, my favourites: Isaac – Jacob's father – and my namesake, Rebekah.

But then even that was taken from me. The leader of the synagogue said that I had an evil spirit in me. It was the spirit that was bending me in two. I was bringing shame upon them all and should stay at home. I sobbed and pleaded but to no avail. My mother explained to me gently and lovingly, it was for the sake of the whole village; for their sake I should stay away.

And so my life closed in around me. For eighteen long years all I saw was the ground and feet. Feet that always hurried past me, lest the spirit that was bending me over should escape and enter them instead.

ON THAT DAY, I KNEW SOMETHING was happening, not because I could see it but because I heard the sound of new feet. Feet I didn't recognise. And then whispers.

The whispers said that Jesus had come.

I'd heard his name before. A few weeks before, my father had returned from his regular trip taking our olive oil to Galilee. He couldn't stop talking about the teacher he had heard who healed the sick, cast out demons and spoke of God's kingdom. He was called Jesus, he'd said.

It was the sabbath day, and from my hunched position close by the wall of our house I saw all the feet in town passing me on the way to the synagogue. As they passed, I heard the chatter.

What would he say, this teacher? Would he tell one of his stories maybe? What would the leader of the synagogue say? Perhaps he'd heal someone?

'Not today,' I heard someone respond. 'He couldn't possibly do that on the sabbath.'

I watched them pass by, one hand on the wall beside me. I felt overwhelmed with the hopelessness of a life I had almost had – but then lost.

Suddenly, unbidden, a long-lost memory slid into my mind. It was of my beloved Lake Galilee, an iridescent blue patch, twinkling in the summer sun on the far horizon, and my sad, lonely heart lifted for a moment. With it came an outrageous idea.

What if I slipped into the synagogue? Perhaps in all the excitement, no one would see me, and I could hear for myself what he had to say.

My feet started moving even before I had fully formed the thought.

I ARRIVED AT THE SYNAGOGUE. There at the back there was just enough space for me and, just as I hoped, all attention was focussed on the man at the front.

The crowd were enrapt, silent, hanging on his every word. I breathed a sigh of relief. I was going to get away with it. No one even noticed I was there.

A moment later, my relief turned to horror. I was wrong. One person had noticed I was there.

Jesus had.

I don't know how. I was right at the back, hidden behind

the entire crowd. But still he saw me, and – even worse – summoned me to him.

I tried to pretend I hadn't heard, but still he called. I shuffled forward, drawn to his voice as though pulled by an invisible cord.

As I made my slow progress to the place where he sat, I saw so many pairs of feet moving as far away from me as they could in that small, crowded place – trying to avoid me touching them as I passed.

And then I saw something different. Something I hadn't seen in eighteen years … a face smiling up at me, his deep brown eyes gleaming with compassion. The great teacher was on his knees before me, looking me in the eye.

'How did you know I was here?' I whispered, my voice trembling.

'I saw you,' he replied softly. 'I see you.'

And then, in a loud voice so everyone could hear, he declared:

'Woman, you are free from your sickness.'

And – just like that – I was.

Like the trees when the wind stops blowing, I stretched back upwards. All around me I saw the astonished faces of the villagers, their mouths hanging open in surprise. The furious face of the leader of the synagogue who looked fit to burst with anger.

But most of all I saw the caring face of the man from Galilee.

I NO LONGER STRETCH UP TALL to catch a glimpse of my beloved Lake Galilee. I see it close by.

I hear its waves lapping on the shores as I sit alongside it in the crowd with my father and mother. Together we hang on every word that Jesus utters.

I no longer stretch up tall to see the lake, but I do stretch up tall. I do it every time those words echo in my heart:

'I see you ... you are free.'

Nine

Martha and Mary of Bethany

MARTHA'S STORY

My name is Martha. I live in Bethany with my sister Mary and our baby brother Lazarus.

When I say 'baby', I should add that he's about eighteen now. But he was born when I was twelve and Mary was ten, so to us he is – and always will be – our baby brother.

Our parents died when Lazarus was still a boy, leaving us to run the farm which spread downwards from Bethany towards Jerusalem. Every time someone calls our hill 'the Mount of Olives' I feel a thrill of pride. We grow some of the olives that gave it its name.

We make a good team, Mary, Lazarus and I, spreading the work out evenly between us.

We first heard Jesus of Nazareth teach when we were visiting our cousins in Galilee a couple of years ago. All three of us hung on his every word. When we talked about it later, we all agreed that what he was saying was so true that it would change our lives for ever.

Now we take every chance we can to listen to him and learn from him, and travel to Galilee whenever we can.

Over time, Jesus developed a particular fondness for Lazarus.

Lazarus is so full of life and energy, it is hard not to care for him. He is the centre of our lives, Mary's and mine. I don't know what we'd ever do without him.

I was just outside the door of our house, checking the olive presses with the servants, when I saw Jesus and his disciples on the road. They had just crested the hill and were coming down the slope towards our farm.

'Mary,' I called. 'does that look like Jesus to you?'

She responded from inside the house.

'You must be seeing things. We'd know if he was coming. Last I heard, he was still in Galilee.'

Just then, Lazarus came back from the olive groves.

'Did you know Jesus was coming?' he asked, looking at the small group of disciples as they made their way down the road towards us.

'Mary,' he called out, 'Jesus is coming!'

That drew Mary out of the house.

I seethed quietly. Of course she would listen to Lazarus and not to me.

Usually we got along very well, Mary and I, but, after all, we are sisters and some days she can be so annoying.

Lazarus and Mary clapped their hands with joy and began running to meet them.

I threw up my hands in horror. Thirteen guests arriving at our house – one of them Jesus – and not a single preparation made.

FORTUNATELY, I HAD SWEPT the floor that morning (as I did every morning).

The house was as clean as it could be in this dusty, baking heat. So, I turned my attention to the food.

I added yeast to a full measure of flour. That should

be enough even for that number of people. I added wood to the fire and started preparing a stew with some of our choicest vegetables and beans.

I sent one servant running to the fruit trees to see what was ripe, and another to the vines to find some grapes. In the outhouse, I unwrapped a cheese I had been saving for a special occasion.

By that time, Jesus and his disciples had reached our door. I went out to greet him and welcome him to our home. Then I rushed straight back to the preparations.

Jesus had given so much to Mary, Lazarus and me. It was a great joy to be able to serve him in return. It would be small thanks for everything he was and did. I was determined that this meal would be the best he had eaten in a long time, even with the little time I had to prepare.

Here we would minister to him, as he ministered to others. There was so much to do.

I remembered we had some dried fish in our store cupboard and some dried fruit, too, so I hurried off to find them. While I was there reaching delicacies from a high shelf I realised that I hadn't seen Mary since Jesus had arrived. I sighed irritably. A bit of help would be nice.

I looked into the room where Jesus sat talking to his disciples. There was Mary, sitting right in front of Jesus as though she was one of his disciples, too.

I TUTTED TO MYSELF and went back to my many tasks, but I couldn't settle to them.

Before I'd seen what Mary was doing, my only thought had been to produce the best, most delicious meal it was possible to produce. Before, I had wanted to prepare something special for Jesus, to show him how grateful I was. Now, resentful thoughts began to develop: she might have helped; she was just sitting there doing nothing; she was so selfish.

I tried to put the thoughts from my mind but every time I pushed them down, they crept back in again.

In the end I could bear it no more. I went and stood at to the side of the disciples, in Mary's eye line.

'Mary,' I hissed.

But she was so engrossed in what Jesus was saying that she didn't hear me.

'Mary,' I said, a little louder. But still she sat there, her face revealing how deeply absorbed she was in Jesus' words.

I waved then, hoping to catch her attention. But it wasn't her attention that I caught. Jesus paused mid-sentence and looked round at me. He raised his eyebrows quizzically.

'Don't you care, Lord,' I asked, 'that my sister has left me to do all the work? Tell her to help me.'

Jesus smiled at me.

'Martha, Martha you are anxious and troubled by so many things, but only one thing is needed. Mary has chosen the better part. It will not be taken away from her.'

I hung my head. His words stung.

I felt my cheeks burning with the reprimand in his

words. All I had wanted was to offer him a gift in return for … well, everything. It didn't seem fair that I would be chastised for it.

It certainly wasn't fair that Mary got to sit there like a proper disciple, while I got to do all the work. After all, I was the one who had heard him first.

When we were in Galilee, I'd gone down to the beach to buy some fish one morning and found a crowd gathered on the shore listening to him.

His words had dropped into my heart like rain in a parched desert, and I knew we all needed to listen to him.

I had rushed to our cousins' house, found Mary and Lazarus and made them come back with me. That's where it had all begun.

So, you see, it really should have been me sitting there at Jesus' feet, taking it all in.

The knot of resentment hardened within me, now including Jesus in its scope, alongside Mary.

When I lifted my head a few moments later, Jesus was looking at me intently. He gestured to the floor by his feet and tipped his head, indicating that I should join Mary and sit.

'There's so much to do.'

The words jumped unbidden to my lips. As they did, Jesus' words of a few minutes earlier echoed in my ears: 'only one thing is needed'.

There was so much that *could* be done. There was a lot that would be nice to have done. There were many things I'd *wanted* to do. But only one thing was needed, and I had nearly overlooked the opportunity to sit at his feet and drink it all in.

Mary turned and shuffled along to make room for me. I admitted defeat and joined her.

WE SAT THERE, Mary and I, among his disciples.

No, I was wrong, we *were* disciples.

Jesus smiled his pleasure at me for joining them and then continued his teaching.

'The kingdom of God is like …'

Within minutes I was drawn in – my mind bubbling with thoughts, my heart burning within me. One by one, my worries dropped away. A deep stillness filled me. I felt whole.

Jesus was right. There was only one thing that was needed.

In all my desire to make things perfect, I had very nearly missed this one, precious moment.

Epilogue

The daughters of Jerusalem

DEBORAH'S STORY

חסד

My name is Deborah. I live in Jerusalem with my two sisters, Esther and Hannah.

We didn't mean to be here today, Esther, Hannah and I. We usually avoid the Roman spectacle of crucifixions.

The Romans love us inhabitants of Jerusalem to watch because they enjoy reminding us of the power they have over us. They especially like us to remember what will happen if we step out of line. The barbarity of it all turns my stomach, so I prefer to stay away.

We ran into the crowd by accident. We thought we had cut through the back streets at just the right point to take us around the crowd that was lined up to jeer today's criminals on their way to their gruesome end. Instead, we ran into the people who were waiting for them to pass.

The crowd was restless, booing and jeering even though there was, as yet, no sign of those who, today, would plod their way to their gory deaths.

By the time we had realised what we had done, we were boxed in by the crowd and had no choice but to wait for it all to be over.

The atmosphere was electric, tense and angry. It felt as though the slightest spark would turn the whole city into rioting chaos.

After a while, I became aware of the women standing next to us.

Their utter silence was in stark contrast to the angry,

heckling crowd. I looked at them. Then I looked again.

They didn't really seem to fit together.

There were a few peasant women dressed as though they would fit in better in a Galilean fishing village.

There was a girl with her mother and father who appeared – though still Galilean – much more affluent.

There was a woman whose hairstyle and clothing made her look like people I'd met who came from Tyre. She was clearly wealthy, and she had her arm around a young girl who looked so much like her that she had to be her daughter.

There was even someone who seemed to dress like the Samaritans did. Surely, I was wrong? Why would a Samaritan be here at the time of our most Holy Festival? She should have been up on Mount Gerizim like the rest of her kind.

Right in the middle of them were two women I did know – Mary and Martha from up on the Mount of Olives – and next to them a woman who looked vaguely familiar but whom I couldn't place.

It was their stillness that was uncanny. As if they were all waiting with bated breath for the worst to happen.

I LEANED FORWARD and waved at Mary.

She turned, her face grey and drawn. I started explaining how we wouldn't usually come to watch a crucifixion but how we'd taken a wrong turning and had ended up here.

She seemed barely able to take it in.

I carried on.

'Why are you here?'

'For Jesus.' Her words were almost inaudible in the hubbub.

'Jesus Barabbas? The bandit?'

'No,' she said, 'they let him go. They're crucifying Jesus of Nazareth in his place.'

I had a vague memory of a conversation we'd had when I saw her last.

'Wasn't he the Rabbi whose teaching you followed?'

The rest of the group had heard our conversation by then.

'We all followed him,' the elegant woman from Tyre explained.

'You seem an odd group,' I said. It was only as the words left my mouth that I realised how rude I sounded. They didn't seem to mind.

'We are,' the woman who seemed vaguely familiar said. 'All we have in common is Jesus, and how he transformed our lives.'

'How did he do that?' My two sisters had been drawn into the conversation now.

So, they told us.

First, Leah, the wife of one of his first followers. Then the woman who looked as though she was a Samaritan (it turned out she was) – Photini her name was.

After her, Dinah, a woman who had bled for twelve years before she met Jesus; and the affluent-looking girl, Tabitha, who everyone had thought had died. Then Elissa, the woman from Tyre, told how he had healed her daughter even though she had not been there in the house with him.

Judith told me about her son who had actually died and was about to be buried, when Jesus brought him to life. As the woman who looked vaguely familiar began to speak, I placed her at last: Menahem's wife, Tamar. She told about how Jesus had saved her from stoning after her disgrace. Finally, there was Rebekah who held herself poised and tall as she told us how she had been bent double for many years. As they spoke, each one of them glowed with passion and life.

They had just finished telling us their stories when some more women arrived. I think I got a bit confused by the introductions, but as far as I could tell most of them were called Mary, and one of them was the mother of this Jesus of Nazareth.

'What did he do to deserve this?' My sisters asked, intrigued.

'He proclaimed good news, healed the sick, cast out demons and taught us how to live life in all its fullness,' Martha replied.

'Why, then, are they crucifying him?' I asked. 'It doesn't make sense.'

'No,' Martha agreed, her heartbreak showing on her face. 'It doesn't make sense at all. Why would you kill the

Saviour of the World?'

'I think,' said Tamar, her forehead wrinkled in thought, 'that he reveals the deepest secrets of our hearts. For some, that is simply too uncomfortable for them to bear.'

All of a sudden, I felt overwhelmed with a sense of doom and hopelessness.

What kind of world was this, that killed a man like this Jesus? What had we become? What would happen to us all?

JUST THEN WE HEARD the rattle and stomp of Roman soldiers – a sound to instil terror into even the most fearless of hearts. It looked as though they had extra soldiers on duty today, so they must have been expecting trouble.

Right behind them came two men. They looked rough types. They had probably been hiding in the hills for years before they were caught.

There was, then, quite a gap.

Finally, I saw a man carrying the third cross. I looked at Mary and Martha surprised. I thought they had said Jesus was from Galilee, this man looked as though he had travelled all the way from North Africa, somewhere like Cyrene.

They shook their heads.

'That's not him.'

'Do you think,' said one of the Marys, 'that they freed him after all?'

Then we heard a low moan from one of the other Marys, the one we'd been told was Jesus' mother. I looked back in the direction of her gaze and saw him.

He was being hauled along between two soldiers. He was in a bad way, blood streaming down his face and back. As he passed us, a scuffle broke out in the crowd behind him, so the soldiers dropped him to the ground, drew their swords and strode over to where the noise was coming from.

Jesus (on his hands and knees now, his strength nearly gone) looked up at the small group of women next to us. For a moment, a look crossed his face. It was a look of such love that my heart trembled within me.

Tamar silently knelt down next to him and wrote in the dust of the ground. I strained to see what she had written. It was a Hebrew word, the word *'ḥesed'* – steadfast love.

He paused just for a moment. Then he nodded, summoned up the last of his strength and struggled to his feet.

My sisters and I followed him a short distance.

By unspoken agreement we began to weep and wail, as we would when someone had died.

After a few stumbling paces, Jesus turned to us.

'Daughters of Jerusalem, do not weep for me but weep for yourselves. There are days coming when the most blessed among you will be childless. If this is what they do when the wood is green, what will they do when it is dry?'

We looked at each other, Esther, Hannah and I. None of us quite understood what he meant.

We stopped in our tracks and watched miserably as his bloodied, broken form shuffled out of sight. I couldn't make sense of what had happened.

All I knew was that it felt as though all the good in the world was being sucked away. It felt as though darkness had won, and light was being extinguished before our very eyes.

If Jesus was right, and this was only the start, how could anyone bear what was to come?

As we watched, we saw the small but resolute band of women following determinedly behind Jesus at a distance. Their unwavering presence gave me a flicker of hope.

The Romans might be about to crucify the source of love and life, but maybe – just maybe – that wouldn't be the end of the story.

NOTES AND RESOURCES

Leah's Story

Bible passages

Mark 1.16-20,29-34
Matthew 13.33

You might find it helpful to know …

Fishing in Galilee

Boats are mentioned regularly throughout the Gospels because, for obvious reasons, they were essential for life around Lake Galilee. In the 1980s, the remains of an ancient boat was discovered on the north-west shore of Galilee, buried in the mud. When it was carbon-dated it was found to come from between the first century BC and the first century AD. It, therefore, allows us to know what the boats used by Simon Peter and Andrew, and James and John, looked like. If you search online for 'Sea of Galilee boat' or 'Jesus boat' you will find lots of images of it.

The nets that the fisherman on Galilee would have used would have included casting nets. These were circular, around 25 feet in diameter, made out of linen and weighted on the edges. There were also large dragnets, some as large as one thousand feet, which would have required more than one boat to set them out at sea. A team of people on shore would then have pulled them in, catching fish on the way.

In Luke's Gospel, Jesus' call of the disciples (Luke 5.1-11) involves a miraculous catch of fish. In Mark's Gospel, the fishing is over and the fishermen are mending their nets. I have used Mark's account in my story here.

Simon Peter's house

Mark's Gospel says that Simon Peter lived in Capernaum but John's Gospel said that they came from Bethsaida (John 1.44), about five miles west along the northern shore of Galilee. One explanation for the discrepancy, which is often offered, is that Simon Peter and Andrew had grown up in Bethsaida but moved their fishing business to Capernaum, which was a large, busy trading town at the time of Jesus.

Christian tradition identifies Simon Peter's house as being right next to the synagogue in Capernaum. Underneath the ruins of a fourth-century church in Capernaum, archaeologists have found the remains of a house from the first century AD. This house was clearly used for Christian worship in the late first century AD (which suggests that its importance was recognised very early in the life of the church). The house was a little bigger than the other houses excavated near it, which suggests that, if this is Simon Peter's house, he was more well-off than his neighbours.

The parable of the woman and the yeast

One of the striking features of the parable of the woman who hid yeast in the flour is the quantity of flour she used. Three measures of flour is over 50 pounds of flour, which would make bread for around 100 people. Underlying the parable is a hint of overwhelming generosity, as well as the ability of the kingdom to flourish and grow.

For reflection

- It is easy to imagine that the disciples who followed Jesus, leaving everything behind, had no families. The story of the healing of Simon's mother-in-law indicates that this is not the case. What impact would Jesus' call to follow him have had on the families of the first disciples?
- One of the most challenging elements of Jesus' teaching is his claim that those who do the will of God are his mother and brother and sister (Mark 3.31-35). How do you react to this teaching? What might it mean for our life of faith today?
- The quantity of bread made by the woman who buried yeast in flour was huge. If the kingdom of heaven is like a woman who makes vast quantities of bread, what does it tell us about God's generosity?

Photini's Story

Bible passage

John 4.1-41

You might find it helpful to know ...

Photini

Photini or Photina is the name given to the Samaritan woman in Eastern Orthodox traditions. Within Orthodox traditions, she is venerated as a saint and considered to be equal to the apostles.

Sychar and Shechem

The village of Sychar, mentioned in John 4.5, could be either the city of Shechem or the small village of Askar. I think the latter is most likely, so imagined Photini as coming to Sychar from the nearby Shechem. Shechem was the first capital of the Northern Kingdom of Israel. Today it lies close to the Palestinian city of Nablus, on the West Bank.

There is no mention in Genesis of a well owned by Jacob, but Genesis 33.18-20 talks about Jacob purchasing a plot of land near Shechem with 100 pieces of silver. It is likely that a well was found in this land. The well can still be visited today. It is ancient and thought to be about 135 feet deep.

Samaritans

Around 800-900 Samaritans still live near the ancient site of Shechem and observe Samaritan beliefs and practices. Their origins are heavily disputed. Samaritans claim that they are the descendants of the tribes of Ephraim and Manasseh and that they split from Judaism during the time of Eli, the priest. Judaism maintains, however, that their origins are much later and date them to the time of the Babylonian exile or even later.

Samaritan beliefs are focused on following the Samaritan Torah, which has a few key differences from the Jewish Torah, and on worship on Mount Gerizim which, they claim, was where a Temple was built by Joshua shortly after God's people entered the promised land. Most important for Samaritans is the Passover sacrifice on Mount Gerizim, which still takes place today.

Wells and their importance

Wells have a deep significance in the Bible beyond their vital role of providing water. They were the symbolic location for betrothals, as can be seen in the stories about Isaac and Rebekah (Genesis 24), Jacob and Rachel (Genesis 29) and Moses and Zipporah (Exodus 2). They were so symbolic of marriage that anyone who saw a man and woman sitting together by a well would immediately think of betrothal.

Divorce laws

Although we don't know what the Samaritan laws of divorce were, there is a lot of evidence of discussion by the Rabbis about Jewish divorce. Divorce was permitted, provided that the man gave to the woman a *'Gett'* or written document that would then allow her to remarry. A key detail here was that a woman was not permitted to provide a *'Gett'*. This could only be done by a man. Famously, the Rabbis disagreed on the conditions that allowed divorce. Rabbi Hillel allowed divorce for any reason, including spoiling a dinner, whereas Rabbi Shammai only permitted it in cases of infidelity.

For reflection

- Does it make any difference to how you think about the conversation between Jesus and the Samaritan woman if she is someone who suffered bereavement and/or was divorced, rather than (as is often assumed) that the fault was entirely hers? Or does it have the same effect no matter whether she was at fault or not?
- The living water that Jesus talked about (4.10) was, of course, metaphorical. What do you think it means? What does it mean to you?
- This is one of the few occasions in the Gospels that Jesus acknowledged directly that he was the Messiah. Why do you think he did that here?

Dinah's Story

Bible passage

Mark 5.24-34

You might find it helpful to know ...

The woman's condition

The words that describe the woman's condition in Greek are even more evocative than the English translation. The first time her condition was mentioned it said that she had 'flowing blood' (v. 25). The second time it was called a 'fountain' or 'spring of blood' (v. 29). There are many conditions that could have caused these symptoms – from endometriosis to fibroids, from non-cancerous polyps to cancer. In addition to bleeding, it is likely that the woman also suffered debilitating cramps and anaemia.

Impurity

A woman was considered ritually impure from the first day of her menstruation until seven full days after the end of her cycle. At that point she could then go to the mikveh (ritual bath) and undertake a ceremony of ritual cleansing.

The law connected to this is known as '*niddah*' which means separation. In other words, the woman is separated from her husband for this time until she is deemed pure once more. Anyone who was ritually pure who touched someone (or something) that was impure would be made impure as well and would need to undergo a ritual purification ceremony.

A woman who bled constantly would never have been able to have the seven clean days after bleeding that were necessary to enable the ritual purification ceremony.

Medicine at the time of Jesus

At the time of Jesus there were two main types of healers: professionals who charged and largely lived in urban areas, and local healers, who depended more on folklore and received wisdom. Physicians were found across the ancient world. Note also that Luke is described as 'the beloved physician' in Colossians 4.14. Those in Egypt and Greece were particularly well-known for their skill in curing diseases. The reference to the woman using up all her money in going to physicians suggests that she had seen professional healers as well as local ones.

For reflection

- One of the features of bleeding for twelve years would have been that people would have avoided touching Dinah to avoid becoming unclean themselves. What would that experience of loneliness have felt like – both the loneliness of being alone and of not being touched for twelve years?
- What emotions would have driven the woman who bled to press into the crowd and touch Jesus? Have you ever had anything approaching that kind of feeling?
- What do you think Jesus meant when he said, 'Your faith has made you well'?

Tabitha's Story

Bible passage

Mark 5.21-24,35-43

You might find it helpful to know ...

The name Tabitha

The name Tabitha is Aramaic and means gazelle. It is the name of an early disciple of Jesus who is mentioned in Acts 9.36-43 (the Greek name we are told was Dorcas). I am not suggesting that the two are the same person. It was a relatively common name. Instead I was playing with the idea that *'talitha'* (little girl, also Aramaic) sounds very like Tabitha. I liked the idea that the girl might have heard one thing and the witnesses another.

Leader of the synagogue

Jairus' importance is emphasized not just by his title of leader of the synagogue, but also by being named in a text where others are not named.

The role of 'leader of the synagogue' means different things in different synagogues. What it probably meant here was that Jairus acted as an administrator, looking after the building and organising services. There is no evidence that he would have been a Priest or Levite. It is interesting that he is described as 'one of the leaders of the synagogue' here. This implies that there was more than one, which was also the case in Acts 13.15.

Bleeding

For more on impurity, see the notes on Dinah's story. Here I was trying to point out that if Tabitha was a 'little girl' of twelve, it probably meant that she had not started menstruation yet. As a result she might be confused by being asked about bleeding and not understand the significance of the question. If she had been menstruating, she should not have been reading the Torah in the synagogue because of the purity laws.

Reclining

Although much of art history depicts Jesus as sitting upright to eat, anyone in the first century would have reclined at the table, their head towards the table and their feet away from it. Jarius, as leader of the synagogue, would almost certainly have followed the custom of reclining to eat.

For reflection

- Jairus could have been forgiven for thinking that Jesus wasted valuable time in stopping to talk to the woman who had been bleeding for twelve years. How might this have felt for him, while he was waiting for Jesus to come with him to his sick daughter?
- In Mark 5, Jairus' daughter was twelve and the woman who bled (Dinah of the previous story) had been ill for twelve years. What does this connection make you think about? Why do you think Mark mentioned it?

- In Mark's account, everyone except Jesus thinks that Jairus' daughter has died. Does it make any difference if she was dead or not? Do you think Jesus knew she wasn't actually dead or thought she was dead but was trying to make a point?

Elissa's Story

Bible passage

Mark 7.24-30

You might find it helpful to know ...

Tyre

The ancient city of Tyre is located on the Mediterranean coast in what is known, today, as Lebanon. It has a long history and was thought to have been founded in the third millennium BC. Like the city often named alongside it, Sidon, Tyre was a city state in Phoenicia, an ancient civilisation which made its fortune through maritime trading. 'Syrophoenician' is a term not widely used in this period, and might have been employed here by Mark to distinguish this part of Phoenicia from the Phoenicians who lived in North Africa at the time (the Libyophoenicians).

In Matthew's account of this same story the woman is called a Canaanite. This was the general term used for a number of ethnic groupings, including the Phoenicians.

Tyrian purple

One of the commodities for which Tyre was most well-known was purple dye. Purple dye first began being made in Phoenicia in around 1200 BC, and the process for making it was a closely guarded secret. The pigment was made from murex shellfish, which could be found on the shores of the Mediterranean. It was very expensive, largely because of the laborious process for extracting the colour from the shellfish, and as a result became a status symbol, worn by kings, military leaders and aristocrats.

Water demons

There was a widespread belief in the ancient world that demons brooded near water. It was believed that if you went near uncovered water at dusk then you would be most at risk for being possessed by a demon. Demon possession (it was believed) could lead to blindness, fits, madness and indeed many other forms of illness.

The trading route

One of the key trading routes in this part of the world was the *Via Maris*, which ran between Egypt, Israel, Tyre, Syria and Mesopotamia. Tyre was a key staging post on this trading route, as indeed was Capernaum. It isn't clear why Jesus went from Capernaum to Tyre (a journey of around fifty miles which would have taken two to three days of walking), but it is likely he went by way of the *Via Maris*.

For reflection

- Why do you think that the Syrophoenician woman didn't bring her daughter with her to be healed? I came up with one theory for this story, but it isn't the only option. What do you think?
- People hold strong opinions on whether they think Jesus was right or wrong in this story. Some think that he was wrong and the Syrophoenician woman corrected him;

others think that he knew exactly what he was doing and was trying to elicit a response from her. What do you think?

- Demons were widely accepted as existing in the ancient world. Today we would identify this kind of experience as some kind of mental illness. Is it helpful or unhelpful to try and translate 'demons' into more modern categories?

Judith's Story

Bible passage

Luke 7.11-17

You might find it helpful to know ...

Location of Nain

The village of Nain lies eight-and-a-half miles south of Nazareth. Its name means 'beauty' or 'loveliness', and probably comes from the view out over the plain of Jezreel to Mount Carmel in the distance. In this story I imagined that Judith might have known Jesus as a child, as the two villages were so close to each other. Although some of the apocryphal gospels have wild tales of Jesus as a child, in the canonical gospels we only hear of one story of Jesus as a child, when he got lost in the Temple (Luke 2.41-52). It is intriguing to think about what it might have been like for people who knew Jesus as a child to encounter him in his ministry.

Joseph as a carpenter

Joseph's trade is traditionally accepted as carpenter. The problem with this is that the Greek word translated '*tekton*' is much less precise than that. It could mean carpenter but it could also mean someone who worked in either metal or stone (or, indeed, all three). A town the size of Nazareth in the first century AD (estimated to be between 100 and 400 people) would be unlikely to support a specialised carpenter. The tradition of Joseph and Jesus being carpenters is a strong one, but the word it is based on is vague. All we can know for certain is that they were skilled artisans.

Burial practices

The bodies of those who had died would have been buried within about eight hours due to the hot climate. The funeral procession that Jesus met would have been taking the body to a tomb outside of the village, possibly a family tomb. Most tombs, especially in this area, would have been caves carved out of a rock.

Once there, the body would have been anointed (most commonly with nard or myrrh) and wrapped in a shroud (if this had not been done at home before they left) and placed on a ledge at the front of the tomb. A large stone would be placed over the entrance and often whitewashed so that those passing by would know it was a tomb. After a year or so, family members would return and collect up the bones of the person, placing them on a ledge further back in the tomb (often in an ossuary) so that the ledge at the front of the tomb was then available for future burials.

For reflection

- We know from the Gospels that the people of Nazareth were sceptical about Jesus and his ministry, and Nain was geographically close to Nazareth so people there may have known Jesus as a child. Why is it that those who have known someone as a child can find it hard to accept them as adults in a different role from what they expected?

- Jesus is described throughout the Gospels as having compassion for those he healed. If we, followers of Jesus, were to develop greater compassion for those we meet what might this look like? What do you understand compassion to be?
- Burial practices have always been important in helping people to grieve those who have died. What do you think are the advantages and disadvantages of the very swift burial practices which were the norm at the time of Jesus, compared to our own much slower process?'

Tamar's Story

Bible passage

John 8.1-11

You might find it helpful to know ...

The history of this passage

This is a very famous story in John so it is therefore surprising to discover that it is not in the earliest manuscripts of John's Gospel. Your English translation has probably put square brackets around it or put it in a smaller font. In some manuscripts it is not there at all; in others it is placed earlier in John (after 7.36) or later (after 21.25). Other manuscripts still have it in Luke's Gospel (after Luke 21.38). From this we can learn that although the story was not included in the earliest manuscripts, early Christians thought it was so important that they made sure it was included somewhere in the gospels.

Adultery and stoning

Deuteronomy 22.23-24 and Leviticus 20.10 both legislate for the stoning of adulterers. It is worth noticing, though, that they declare that both the man and the woman should be stoned, not the woman alone as is suggested by this passage.

The Rabbis discussed this practice at length and put around it such stringent conditions that most scholars think that the practice happened rarely, if at all. Given this, it is clear that the Scribes and the Pharisees were asking Jesus a trick question, designed to ascertain his knowledge of the law and Rabbinic discussion about it. Jesus' response to this knotty issue is unique in this period.

Writing on the ground

The fact that we do not know what Jesus wrote on the ground in response to the accusations has led to extensive speculation about what it might have been. Some suggest that he wrote Jeremiah 17.13: 'All who forsake you shall be put to shame; those who turn away from me shall be recorded in the underworld for they have forsaken the fountain of living water, the LORD.' Others wonder if he was writing out the sins of those accusing the woman, or maybe the
Ten Commandments.

It is an interesting exercise to reflect on what you think he might have written.

Condemn/judge

In the NRSV Bible translation, when Jesus talks to the woman he asks her first whether anyone has condemned her (8.10) and then says he won't condemn her either (8.11). Actually the Greek words here are slightly different. The first time condemn is used, the meaning is closer to sentence to death (*katakrinō*). The second time, a simpler version of the same word is used (*krinō*) which means to judge. This feels important. They did not sentence her to death, but Jesus wasn't even going to judge her.

For reflection

- The scribes and Pharisees were clearly trying to trap Jesus in this story. What do you think they were trying to get him to say?
- No one knows what Jesus wrote on the ground. I imagined that Jesus might have written 'steadfast love' and 'truth'. What do you imagine he might have written?
- Jesus tells the woman that he does not condemn/judge her. What might the world be like if we followed this example a little more closely?

Rebekah's Story

Bible passage

Luke 13.10-17

You might find it helpful to know ...

Gamla

Luke just locates this healing story in 'one of the synagogues' so I took the artistic liberty of moving it into the hills around Galilee. Gamla was an ancient Jewish city, today located in the Golan Heights. It is on a camel-shaped ridge in the mountains (hence its name Gamla, the Aramaic word for camel) and is most well known for being a rebel stronghold during the Jewish War in AD 67. After an extended siege, Vespasian's troops eventually captured the town and massacred its inhabitants, though many committed suicide in an attempt to avoid being killed by the Romans.

One of the oldest synagogues has been found in Gamla, and it is true that you can see the Sea of Galilee twinkling in the distance from certain parts of the town.

A spirit that had crippled her

There is a lot of discussion about whether this miracle of Jesus falls more into the category of healing or exorcism. It is certainly true that the word demon isn't used in this passage. As a result, the word 'spirit' could be closer to 'condition' than to demon. It is nevertheless interesting to notice that the woman's condition was attributed to an external force. Although very few people believe that spirits or demons cause illness, many people still ask what they've done to deserve what has happened to them.

Leader of the synagogue

The same word is used for leader of the synagogue here as in the story of the healing of Jairus' daughter (see Tabitha's story above). In other words, this was an administrator whose job was the good running of the synagogue. Hence his outrage at the breaking of Sabbath law.

Healing on the Sabbath

One of the times that Jesus most often ended up in conflict with the Jewish leaders around him was when he healed on the Sabbath. Jewish law strictly forbids all forms of work on the Sabbath. The exception to this is where there is a life-threatening situation. None of the conditions which Jesus healed on the Sabbath fall into the category of life-threatening. The woman who was bent double could just as easily have waited a day to be healed. It is clear, therefore, that Jesus was making a strong point by healing in this way. His point was that life-giving acts should be done whenever they are needed, Sabbath or not.

For reflection

- Although possession by a demon or spirit is often associated today with what we would define as mental illness, it is interesting that the woman's physical condition is attributed to a 'spirit' in this story. Why do you think people did this at the time of Jesus?

- My imagining that Jesus got to his knees to look into the woman's face when he healed her is fanciful, but not impossible. Have you had an experience in which you have felt 'seen' – either by God or by someone else?
- In many healing stories the word used is 'saved'. Here it is 'freed'. The condition had bound her for many years and now she was free. What does the language of 'freedom' make you think about in this story?

Martha's Story

Bible passage(s)

Luke 10.38-42
(You could also read John 11.1-44 if you want to read the other story about the family, too)

You might find it helpful to know ...

The Mount of Olives and Bethany

The Mount of Olives is a mountain ridge just east of the Old City of Jerusalem. Bethany is located on the south-eastern slope of the Mount of Olives a couple of miles from Jerusalem.

At the time of Jesus, olive groves covered the slopes of the mountain, giving it its name. It is, therefore, not unlikely to imagine that people living in Bethany were involved in the cultivation of olives. The garden of Gethsemane lies at the foot of the Mount of Olives. Its name comes from the Hebrew '*Gat-shemanim*' which means olive press and was (as its name suggests) where the olives grown on the mountain were brought to be pressed.

One of the intriguing questions that emerges from this story is how Jesus knew Mary, Martha and Lazarus. According to Matthew and Mark, Jesus did not travel to Jerusalem until the last week of his life, though John has Jesus going every year for the Passover. Luke's account here reflects Jesus' very slow progress to Jerusalem that began in Luke 9.51, when Jesus set his face to go to Jerusalem. The account of the raising of Lazarus in John 11.1-44 indicates that Jesus not only knew the family but knew them very well (and was particularly fond of Lazarus). The options, therefore, are that either Jesus came to Jerusalem much more regularly than is recorded in Matthew, Mark and Luke, or that Martha, Mary and Lazarus got to know him in Galilee.

Food at the time of Jesus

The food that would have been eaten at the time of Jesus would have consisted predominantly of bread, fruit, nuts and olives, lentils, beans and chickpeas, and cheese. Those living near Lake Galilee would have had a steady supply of fresh fish, but a village like Bethany, which was 90 miles from the lake, would have had to rely on salted or dried fish. Meat was rare and usually only consumed after sacrifices in the Temple.

Much ministry

The NRSV Bible describes Martha as being distracted by 'many tasks'. The implication is that she was doing things that were not very important. The Greek word used here, though, is '*diakonia*', normally translated 'ministry' or 'service'. The ministry of hospitality was vital in this period. Jesus' point was not that Martha was doing something unimportant, but that she was missing a particular opportunity that would not often be available to her.

For reflection

- How do you think Jesus knew Mary, Martha and Lazarus?
- What difference does it make to know that Martha was busy with 'much ministry'? Does this change the emphasis of the story at all? (It may not!)
- What do you think Jesus' message to Martha was in this story? And to Mary?

Deborah's Story

Bible passage

Luke 23.26-30

You might find it helpful to know …

Public crucifixions

The public nature of crucifixions was their point as far as the Romans were concerned. The purpose of them was as much to instil fear, and hence control, over the population as it was to execute criminals, rebels and slaves. The *Pax Romana* (the peace of Rome) was enforced using barbaric techniques, one of which was crucifixion. As a result, the Romans tried to make crucifixions as public as possible.

Simon of Cyrene

At the start of this passage, soldiers seized a man called Simon of Cyrene and forced him to carry Jesus' cross. In Mark's Gospel he is identified as the father of Alexander and Rufus (Mark 15.21) which suggests that his sons became a part of the later Christian community. Cyrene was an Ancient Greek colony, from around the seventh century BC. Between 67 and 30 BC, it became part of the Roman province of Crete and Cyrenaica.

'Daughters of Jerusalem'

The phrase first occurs in the Bible in the Song of Solomon, where it is used seven times (1.5; 2.7; 3.5; 3.10; 5.8,16; 8.4) as an address, urging the daughters of Jerusalem not to stir up or awaken love until it is ready. The implication, therefore, is that the daughters of Jerusalem were young, unmarried women. This resonance makes sense here in this passage, too, where Jesus says that those who are childless are blessed.

Jesus Barabbas

Only Matthew's Gospel gives Barabbas a first name (Jesus), and only then in some manuscripts, not all of them. The Early Church Fathers, however, made much of his name on the grounds that the people were given the choice between two Jesuses: one who took life, and one who gave it.

Little is known about Barrabas beyond the descriptions of him in each of the Gospels. Matthew describes him as a 'notorious prisoner' (Matthew 27.16). Mark says that he was 'was in prison with the rebels who had committed murder during the insurrection' (Mark 15.7). Luke describes Barrabas as 'a man who had been put in prison for an insurrection that had taken place in the city, and for murder' (Luke 23.19), and John 18.40 states that he was a bandit.

'Many women were also there ...'

All the Gospels describe women being present at the crucifixion. Matthew names those present as Mary Magdalene, Mary the mother of James and Joseph, and the mother of the sons of Zebedee (Matthew 27.55-56). Mark names them as Mary Magdalene, Mary the mother of James the younger and of Joses, and Salome (Mark

15.40-41). Luke gives no names of the women present, and John says that three Marys were present: Mary the mother of Jesus, Mary, wife of Clopas, and Mary Magdalene (John 19.25).

(In the first volume in this series, *Women of Holy Week*, I included accounts of the events of Holy Week and Easter as seen through the eyes of some of the women named as present at the crucifixion.)

Matthew, Mark and Luke all record, however, that women who followed him from Galilee were also present. Although we don't know who they were, it is not impossible that at least some of the women named in this volume were among them.

What will they do when the wood is dry?

Jesus' slightly enigmatic parting question to the women (Luke 23.31) is usually taken to refer to the Jewish War that took place between AD 67 and 70. If this is how the Romans treated someone they believed to be innocent but was inconvenient, what would happen when the whole nation rebelled against them? The implication is that the whole country would go up in flames.

For reflection

- Think about who might have been present in Jerusalem for the Passover. We know that Jesus and the twelve were there, but also that Mary the mother of Jesus, Mary Magdalene and a few other named women were present. Alongside them other unnamed women are also referred to. Who might they have been?

- One of the most hopeful features of the crucifixion accounts is that the women didn't abandon Jesus but were present right up to his burial. What glimmers of hope does their presence provide? Why do you think they stayed?

www.ingramcontent.com/pod-product-compliance
Lightning Source LLC
LaVergne TN
LVHW071255230826
846271LV00033BA/295
9781781405260